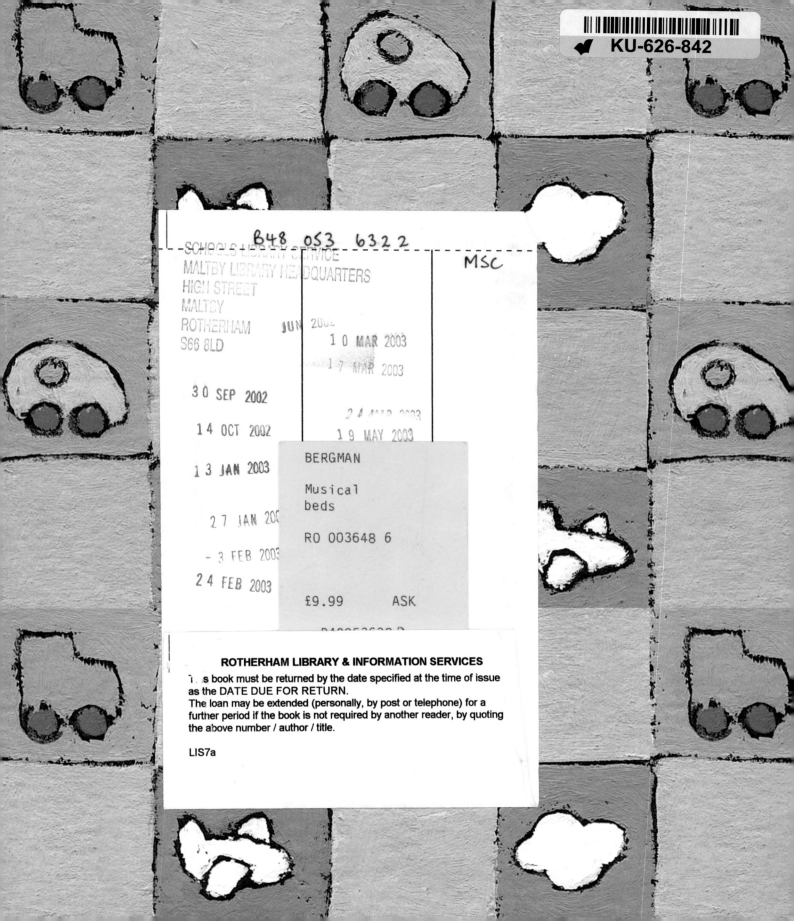

For Marissa, Eva and Jonathan
but especially for Martin and parents everywhere
M.B.

For Maura, Linde and Hilke
M.P.

Musical Beds

Written by Mara Bergman
Illustrated by Marjolein Pottie

Simon & Schuster
London • New York • Sydney

Josie could not sleep.

The moon was too bright.

The old tree shivered and shook in the light.

"Daddy!" she called. "Come here quick!

There's a witch in my room!"

Rosie could not sleep.

The room was too cool.

and something called

Whooo! Whooo! Whooo!

"Daddy!" she called. "Come here quick!

There's a ghost in my room!"

Dad came upstairs.
"Don't worry," he said.
"It's only the wind
whistling through the apple tree."

He shut the window tight
and kissed Rosie good night.
"Go to sleep now," Dad said.

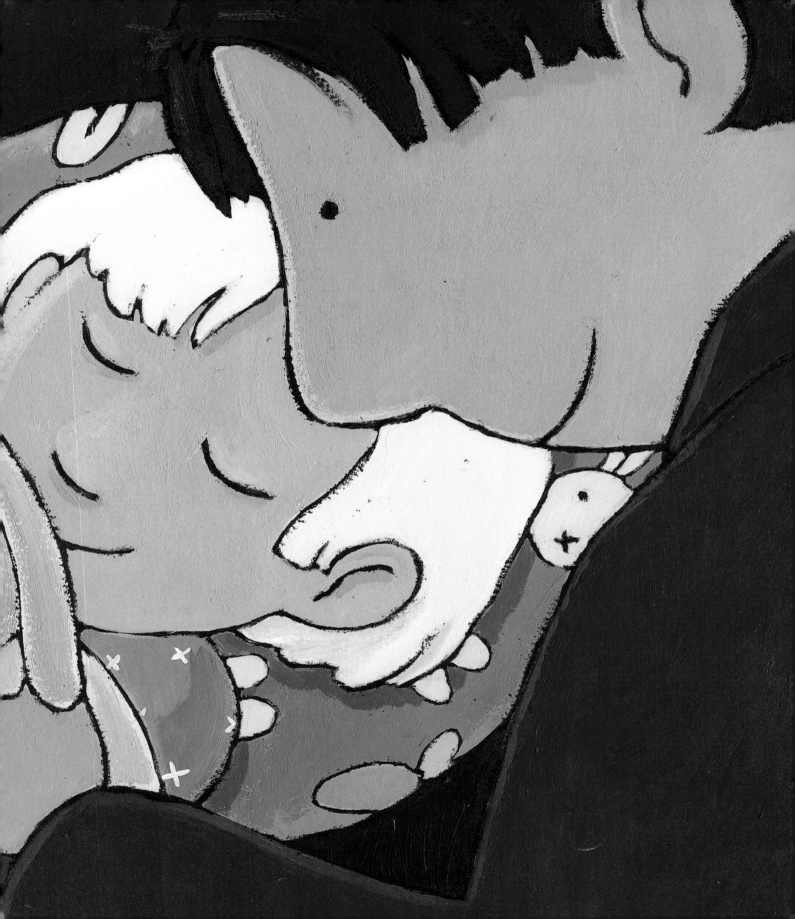

But Rosie could not sleep
so she slipped across the hall
to Mum and Dad's room.
The room was cozy
and there were no scary noises.

Rosie slipped into the big bed and
crawled between the warm sheets.
Soon she was fast asleep.

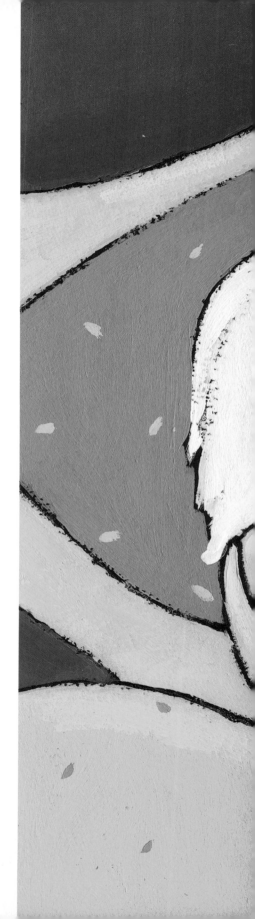

Little Rick could not sleep.
"I'm thirsty!" he called.

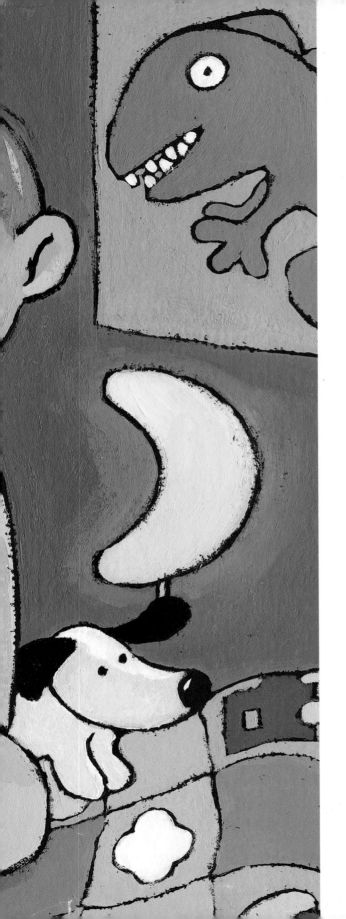

No one answered
and no one came
so he bounced

down the

stairs on

his bottom.

Dad gave little Rick a glass of water,
then carried him back to bed.

"Go to sleep now," Dad said.

It was Dad's turn to sleep.
There was no room in the big bed
so he went to Rosie's bed,
in the bottom bunk.
He was reading his book when . . .

Little Rick came in.
"Daddy, I can't sleep, I'm lonely!"
Little Rick climbed into bed next
to Dad . . .

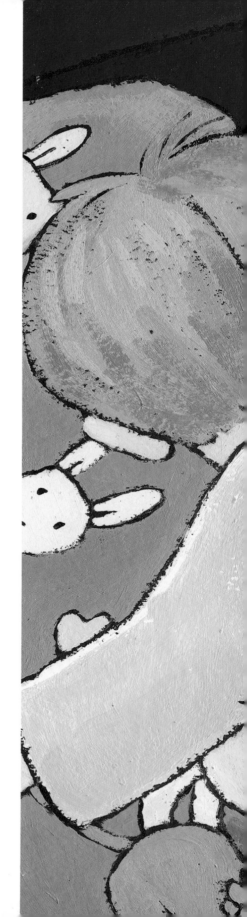

. . . and soon he was fast asleep.

But Dad could not sleep!
Little Rick kept kicking him
and pushing him.
Dad could not sleep
so he climbed to the top bunk.

But it was full of cuddlies and
books and pointy puzzle pieces
and besides . . .
Dad wanted to sleep in his own bed.

There was only one thing to do!

First he carried Little Rick
back to his own room.
He put Doggy and Monkey and Lion
all around him
so he wouldn't be lonely.
Little Rick slept, snug as a snail.

Then Dad carried Josie back to her bed.

There were no scary shadows and no witches.

Josie slept, cozy as a caterpillar.

Next, Dad carried Rosie back to her bed.
There were no scary noises and no ghosts.
Rosie slept, quiet as a carrot.

Then Dad read in
bed for a few minutes
before he, too, fell
fast asleep . . .
tired as a turnip.

When Mum came home
she gave everyone a
good night kiss.
First Josie, who was cosy
in the top bunk,
just where *she* belonged.

Then Rosie, who was quiet
in the bottom bunk,
just where *she* belonged.

Then Little Rick, snug
in his own room,
just where *he* belonged.

Then Mum got into her bed
next to Dad, feeling very pleased
that everyone would sleep,
comfy as kittens,
peaceful as pandas . . .

. . . at least until morning!

Arctic Ocean

Europe

Asia

Africa

typhoon area

Indian Ocean

willy willy area

Australia

roaring forties

Antarctica

Credits
Illustrations
Peter Holt pages 10-11, pages 36-37
Ivan Lapper pages 22-23, pages 24-25,
pages 28-29, pages 30-31, pages 32-33,
pages 38-39
Donald Myall pages 12-13
Jim Robins pages 4-5, page 6 (bottom),
page 7 (bottom), page 10, page 14 (top),
page 16 (left), page 22 (left),
page 23 (right), page 34 (bottom)
Tom Stimpson pages 2-3, page 15,
pages 16-17, page 19, pages 26-27,
pages 34-35, end sheets
Peter Visscher page 19 (bottom),
pages 20-21, pages 26-27 (bottom),
page 27 (top), page 36 (bottom)
Tony White page 2 (left), page 5 (right),
page 6 (left), page 7 (right),
pages 14-15 (bottom), page 18,
page 28 (left), page 32 (bottom)
Elizabeth Wood page 4 (left), pages 8-9,
page 11 (right), page 17 (top),
page 25 (right), page 26 (bottom),
page 31 (right), page 40 (bottom)
Cover illustration Terry Pastor

Editor Sue Tarsky
Designer Judith Escreet

Picture researcher Wendy Boorer
Photography
page 8 Tim Pearcey Travel Ltd; page 17
Trevor Page/Alan Hutchison Library; page 20
(bottom) NASA; pages 20-21 NOAA/American
Red Cross; page 25 Elizabeth Photo Library;
page 26 P. Fitzgerald; page 29 Press
Association; page 33 Institute of Geological
Sciences; page 34 (left) Crown Copyright;
pages 34-35 Novosti; page 35 (right) Kevan
Barker/Oxfam; page 37 Novosti

Published 1981 by Methuen Children's Books Ltd,
11 New Fetter Lane, London EC4P 4EE
in association with
Walker Books, 17-19 Hanway House,
Hanway Place, London W1P 9DL

© 1981 Walker Books Ltd
First printed 1981
Printed and bound by
L.E.G.O., Vicenza, Italy

British Library Cataloguing in Publication Data
Ford, Adam
    Weather watch.
    1. Weather - Juvenile literature
    I. Title
    551.5   QC981.3
    ISBN 0-416-05670-9

Contents

WEATHER WATCH

Written by
Adam Ford

Consultant Paul Arthur
Meteorologist

METHUEN/WALKER BOOKS
London · Sydney · Auckland · Toronto

Weather at work

The wind and the rain, sunshine and clouds, floods and droughts, snow and hail, heat and cold are some of the things people mean when they talk about the weather. The climate is the normal pattern of weather conditions that people can expect in any particular place throughout the year.

Distribution of the Sun's heat

The Sun produces the heat that stirs the atmosphere and makes all our weather. More energy reaches Earth from the Sun in one minute than all of mankind uses in a year.

Earth does not trap all the Sun's heat, however. A lot of it is reflected straight back into space by clouds, or by snow and ice at the polar ice caps. These conditions vary from day to day and, consequently, so does the world's weather.

Even a volcano may cut down the amount of solar heat, or radiation, that reaches the Earth's surface, by hurling several billion tonnes of dust high into the atmosphere. No one is yet sure how much effect volcanoes have on the weather, or how much heat is lost to Earth because of the dust.

The world's weather is further complicated because the Earth's axis is tilted as the Earth spins daily on its yearly orbit of the Sun. This means that for half the year, one hemisphere is tilted towards the Sun, while the other hemisphere is tilted away from it. As the Earth orbits the Sun, the positions of the hemispheres reverse, causing the change from one season to another.

The greenhouse effect, named because a greenhouse works on the same principle, also influences the world's weather and heat.

Losing heat
Clouds reflect much of the Sun's heat back into space, stopping it from reaching the Earth.

Fresh snow and large sheets of ice at the north and south poles reflect about 85% of the Sun's heat into space.

Ash and dust thrown up by an erupting volcano may block more of the Sun's heat, reflecting it back into space.

Today the Sahara Desert is a wasteland of sand and rock, permanently shimmering in the intense heat of the Sun.

Water vapour and carbon dioxide in the Earth's atmosphere trap some of the Sun's heat like a greenhouse, keeping both the Earth's atmosphere and surface air warm.

The oceans also affect the distribution of heat. Warm sea-water from the tropics circulates slowly into cooler regions. The Gulf Stream, for instance, brings warm water from the Gulf of Mexico to the coastal waters of parts of Europe, therefore giving a milder climate to those areas.

Changes of weather and climate

Mankind has always had problems with weather and climatic changes. About 8,000 years ago, the area now known as the Sahara Desert was covered in vegetation. People lived and hunted there. We know this because of the cave paintings in Tassili, in the middle of the Sahara. They were painted when the Sahara was green, and show village communities and hunters. The climate of this area has changed since then, and is now ruled by drought. Today, climatic changes and freak weather conditions continue to surprise people round the world.

The atmosphere

Air is made up of a mixture of gases. The most important gases are nitrogen, oxygen, carbon dioxide and water vapour. Almost all of our weather is in a layer called the troposphere, which extends from ground level to about 15km (9km at the poles). From 15km to 50km is the stratosphere. From 50km to an indefinite height is the ionosphere, beyond which is empty space.

Air pressure

You may not feel it, but air has weight. A vertical column of air, above an umbrella for instance, stretching up to the outer limits of Earth's atmosphere, weighs about 10 tonnes. You do not feel this weight because air behaves like a fluid, spreading out its load in all directions – up and down and sideways. This force is called pressure. Air pushes down on the umbrella with equal pressure from all directions, just as a fluid would.

There are more than five-and-a-half thousand million million tonnes of our atmosphere enveloping the whole planet. Normally, we are not aware of the pressure because it is balanced by an equal amount of pressure inside our bodies, pushing out.

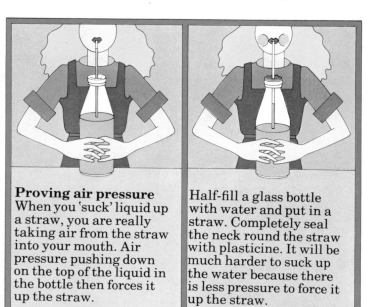

Proving air pressure
When you 'suck' liquid up a straw, you are really taking air from the straw into your mouth. Air pressure pushing down on the top of the liquid in the bottle then forces it up the straw.

Half-fill a glass bottle with water and put in a straw. Completely seal the neck round the straw with plasticine. It will be much harder to suck up the water because there is less pressure to force it up the straw.

Atmospheric pressure is measured in millibars. At sea level, the pressure is about 1,013 millibars – a little more than 1kg of pressure per sq cm.

Measuring air pressure

Barometers measure air pressure. Most barometers today are called aneroids, which means 'non-liquid'. The aneroid is a small box that has been partially emptied of air, and is sensitive to pressure changes in the atmosphere. It registers these changes with a needle that swings across a dial.

The barometer helps meteorologists (people who study the science of weather) to make weather forecasts. Changes in atmospheric pressure, due to constantly moving air, lead to changes in the weather.

Air pressure systems

In a high pressure system, which is called an anticyclone, a barometer might read 1,040 millibars. In a low pressure system, called a depression or cyclone, pressure might drop to 950 millibars. Places with the same pressures are joined together on weather maps by lines called isobars. Iso means 'the same'. Fine, dry weather is associated with anticyclones, and troubled, wet weather usually accompanies cyclonic depressions.

Effects of pressure
The pressure of gas in a balloon equals that of air outside it at ground level. As it rises, the air pressure lessens, so the balloon expands until it finally bursts.

You may get a popping sensation in your ears when you are in a car going down a long, steep hill. This is because your body's internal pressure adjusts to the change in external air pressure.

A house may explode in a tornado. Air pressure inside stays the same, while pressure outside drops quickly as the storm's centre goes by. This causes the house to explode.

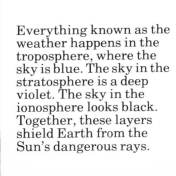

Everything known as the weather happens in the troposphere, where the sky is blue. The sky in the stratosphere is a deep violet. The sky in the ionosphere looks black. Together, these layers shield Earth from the Sun's dangerous rays.

Air on the move

Hot air rises
During the day, air over land gets warm before air over water. The warm air expands, becomes lighter and rises.

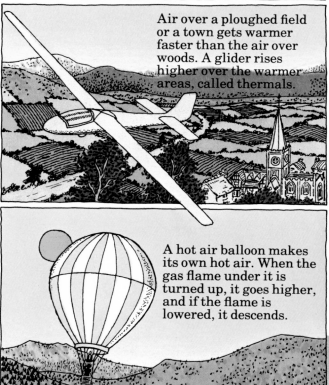

Air over a ploughed field or a town gets warmer faster than the air over woods. A glider rises higher over the warmer areas, called thermals.

A hot air balloon makes its own hot air. When the gas flame under it is turned up, it goes higher, and if the flame is lowered, it descends.

Wind is air moving from one place to another, whether the air is a light evening breeze or a roaring hurricane.

Air travels long distances. When Mt Helens erupted in 1980, air carried volcanic dust from the west coast of the USA to Europe. Wind has also borne red sand from the Sahara Desert to Britain.

The cause of wind

Heat from the Sun is a driving force behind all the world's winds. The Sun warms the seas and the land, and they in turn warm the atmosphere above them. The air then begins to circulate because air expands when warmed, gets lighter and so rises. The atmosphere tries to balance air distribution.

Where winds are born

Warm air rising at the equator contributes to winds circulating round the Earth. As the warm air rises, cooler masses of air move in from the northern and southern hemispheres to replace it. These cooler masses are called the trade winds.

Winds are also born near the sea, where their directions may change from day to night. On a summer day, land heats up faster than the sea. Air above the land rises.

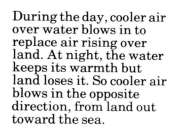

During the day, cooler air over water blows in to replace air rising over land. At night, the water keeps its warmth but land loses it. So cooler air blows in the opposite direction, from land out toward the sea.

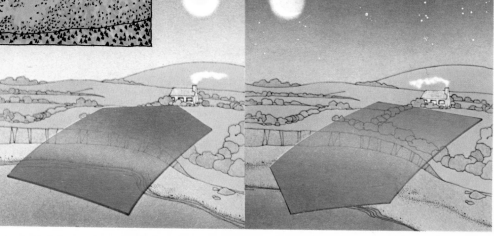

Cooler air from the sea then flows in to replace it. At night, land cools quickly, but the sea retains its warmth and so the movement is reversed.

The same thing happens seasonally above oceans and continents. These seasonal winds are called monsoons. They are very dramatic in Asia, where moisture-laden air from the Indian Ocean or China Seas sweeps inland in summer, bringing very heavy rainfall. During winter, the monsoons blow in the opposite direction, from land to sea.

Wind direction affects weather

Winds are named after the directions from which they blow. Westerlies, for instance, blow from the west, and easterlies come from the east.

Weather is very dependent on wind direction. Some winds are cool rivers of air moving down from polar regions, while others are warm air from the tropics. Air that comes from over a continent is dry and may be hazy with dust, while air from above an ocean is moist and brings rain and clouds.

When a warm mass of air invades a mass of cooler air, it is called a warm front. When a cold mass of air moves to meet a warm mass of air, it is called a cold front.

Wind direction
Weather vanes turn with the wind. So the way a vane points is also the direction from which the wind blows.

Smoke from open chimneys is a good indication of which way wind is blowing, because the smoke is carried along by the wind.

You can tell the wind's direction by holding up a wet finger in the air. It will get cold on the same side as that from which the wind is blowing.

A wind sock is a tube of material that billows out to face downwind at the top of a pole. Wind socks are used mainly by airport authorities.

Jet streams are winds that circle the Earth, moving from west to east high in the atmosphere. Since they blow at about 250 km per hour, they can increase or decrease the speed of aeroplanes, depending on their directions of flight.

Temperature

The temperature of an area depends on several things. The most important is latitude – a measurement in degrees of how far north or south of the equator a place is. The equator is at 0°, the north and south poles are each at 90° and mid-latitudes are areas that lie half-way between.

At the equator, the noon Sun shines from high in the sky. In high latitudes at the polar regions, the Sun is always so near the horizon that very little of its heat reaches the frozen ground. Equatorial areas collect more of the Sun's heat than anywhere else in the world.

Thermometers

Air temperature is measured by thermometers. Temperatures are recorded in the shade, not in direct sunlight. Two scales of measurement are used. On the Fahrenheit scale water boils at 212°F and freezes at 32°F. On the Centigrade, or Celsius, scale water boils at 100°C and freezes at 0°C.

Comfortable weather conditions depend on humidity (the amount of water vapour in the air) as well as on temperature. A summer's day can be uncomfortable if it is very humid. People stay cool by sweating.

The temperature of the Riviera in France is affected by its closeness to cool sea breezes, the shelter it gets from the nearby mountains, and its low level. For about every 140 m above sea level, the temperature drops 1°C.

Equatorial and tropical rain climates have hot sunshine, constant high temperatures and heavy rain regularly, so plant life is profuse. The seasonal monsoon areas of China, India and south-east Asia have this kind of climate.

Warm tropical air and cool polar air meet in temperate areas. The winter season, which may be five months long, is noticeably different from the summer season, which may be very warm. Deciduous trees grow in these climates.

In wet, cold climates cool summers are followed by cold, snowy winters. Most water falls in the form of snow. There are long hours of daylight in mid-summer. Grassland grows in warmer areas, and pine forests in the colder ones.

As water on our skins is absorbed into the air, it takes heat from our bodies. On a very humid day, this happens slowly because the air already holds almost all the moisture it can. We are not cooled as well as on a less humid day, and believe the day is hotter than it is. People are not good thermometers!

The world divided

Temperatures help define climates. A German biologist named Köppen devised one system that divides world climates into five categories, each based on temperature.

Firstly, there are the equatorial and tropical rain climates in Africa, South America and the Far East. The dry climates in broad areas on either side of the equator form the second category. Thirdly, there are temperate climates with no great temperature extremes, in mid-latitudes of both hemispheres. Parts of Europe, the USA and Australia are included in this group. Fourthly are snowy, cold climates of large continents in higher latitudes – parts of northern Europe and Canada. Lastly are polar climates, the Arctic and Antarctic, as well as northern Canada, the USSR and Asia.

Dry climates, such as large deserts round the world, have temperatures that are usually high throughout the year. The warm, dry air and the strong Sun mean that rainfall here is rare, usually coming only from summer storms.

In polar climates in high latitudes it is very cold and dry all year, even in the short and sunny summers. These areas may be covered in sheets of ice. In these polar climates, very few plants can survive the frozen conditions.

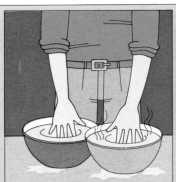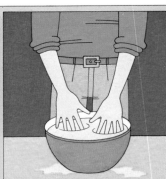

A human thermometer
Fill one bowl with cold water, a second with warm water and another with water as hot as you can bear. Put one hand in the cold water and the other in the hot water for one minute.

Prove that people are not good thermometers by plunging both hands into the warm water. The hand that was in the bowl of hot water will feel cold, while the hand that was in the bowl of cold water will seem warm.

Water on the move

Water is always on the move. In its liquid form it runs down hills as streams or rivers. Even in solid form it creeps slowly down from cold mountains as glaciers of ice. Water moves fastest in its gaseous form of invisible water vapour, mixing with the other gases in the atmosphere. On a summer's day, an average-sized room contains about four-and-a-half litres of water suspended invisibly in the air.

The forms of water

Basically, water is made up of two substances: hydrogen and oxygen. Two particles of hydrogen joined to one particle of oxygen make one molecule of water.

Water molecules hold together tightly as a solid if the temperature drops below 0°C (freezing point), as in ice cube trays in a freezer. Above 0°C, the molecules hold together more loosely, so the solid melts into a liquid. Above 100°C (boiling point), water turns into a vapour because the molecules become very active and go their own ways, as from a kettle left on the boil.

The forms of water
In its gaseous state, water is invisible as water vapour, evaporating from the Earth or being exhaled by plants.

In its liquid state, water becomes visible again as clouds or fog. It may then fall back to the Earth as large drops of rain, fine drizzle, or snow or hail.

In its solid state, water returns to the Earth as snow crystals, hailstones or frost. The ground temperature must be below 0°C for frost.

Liquid water also becomes vapour below boiling point. Water molecules escape from liquid, slowly mixing with air, all the time. This process is called evaporation.

The hydrocycle

Evaporation is part of the regular recycling of the Earth's water supplies. Water is continuously evaporating from seas, rivers and ponds, as well as from wet soil and pavements. During one year many hundreds of billions of tonnes of water vapour rise up silently into the atmosphere. It then returns to Earth in various forms, such as rain or snow. This continuous movement of water is called the hydrocycle.

Plants exhale water

Another route that water takes up into the atmosphere is through plants. They breathe out water vapour through their leaves. This is known as transpiration.

Plants use water from the soil to carry minerals that they need for growth. It travels up from the soil and through their stems to the leaves. Most of the water then passes out through the leaves. A deciduous tree, such as an oak, transpires as much as three-quarters of a tonne of water in one summer's day. A maize plant passes 200 litres through its leaves in one season. An invisible fountain of water vapour is continuously moistening the Earth's atmosphere.

Water from rivers, soil and plants rises into the atmosphere all the time. It may return to Earth as rain or snow.

Water from a plant
Leaves of plants breathe out water vapour. You can test this on a sunny day. Tie a clear plastic bag round a bunch of leaves at the end of a branch. Within 24 hours you will see that the inside of the bag is wet.

Clouds

A cloud is made up of billions of tiny ice or water droplets. There are basically three types of clouds: *Cirrus*, *Stratus* and *Cumulus*. All clouds give clues to weather.

The height of a cloud refers to the height of the base, and so is a measure of how low the cloud comes to the ground.

Cirrus are the highest common clouds, between 5,000 m and 13,700 m high. They are made of small ice crystals because at these great heights the temperature is always well below freezing. After a period of fine weather, they may indicate the approach of wet, stormy weather.

Ordinary *Cirrus* clouds look like white horse tails against blue sky. High winds may flick back the ends.

Cirro stratus clouds mean that rain or snow is probably on the way within 24 hours, especially if the sheet of cloud thickens, slowly reducing the Sun's light.

Cirro stratus clouds cover the sky as a thin, milky veil. A halo will be seen round the Sun or round the Moon.

Cirro cumulus clouds appear either when a warm front is coming with rain, or before a storm. Often the name 'mackerel sky' is given to this kind of cloud formation.

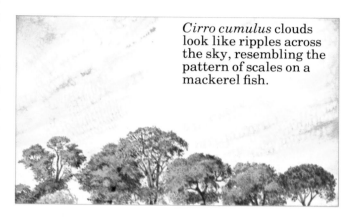

Cirro cumulus clouds look like ripples across the sky, resembling the pattern of scales on a mackerel fish.

Alto means 'medium'. *Alto cumulus* and *Alto stratus* vary in height between 2,000 m and 7,000 m. They are made of water droplets or ice crystals, depending on the height of the clouds. When the heaps of *Alto cumulus* grow, rain and thunderstorms may be approaching.

Alto cumulus clouds appear as grey streaks and patches, sometimes mixed with *Cumulus*-type heaps.

If *Alto stratus* clouds thicken and spread across the sky, rain is likely. These clouds form in layers, not heaps.

Alto stratus clouds cover the sky with patchy layers of grey, through which a watery Sun can be seen.

Nimbo stratus clouds cover the sky with a grey cloud layer. The Sun cannot be seen through these clouds.

Cumulus means 'heap', which is what these clouds look like, floating in the sky between 460 m and 2,000 m. A procession of them stretching across the sky with the wind is called a street of *Cumulus*. These clouds look as light as cotton wool, but each may hold 1,000 tonnes of water. If they get smaller, fair weather is indicated.

Stratus clouds vary between ground level and 460 m. They often produce light rain in the form of drizzle.

Cumulus clouds have clearly defined outlines. They are the small, fluffy clouds that drift across a summer sky.

Stratus clouds cover the sky with a low grey layer. When they are at ground level, these clouds are called fog.

Nimbo stratus clouds may come down as low as 900 m. They often develop from *Alto stratus*. *Nimbo* means 'rain', and snow or rain falls from these clouds almost continuously. When it rains for hours on a dark day, the cloud layer is probably *Nimbo stratus*. The base of this layer is ragged.

Strato cumulus are between 460 m and 2,000 m. They are not usually rain clouds, but might produce light snow in cold weather.

Strato cumulus clouds appear as irregular folds and layers, uneven patterns and patches, running across the sky.

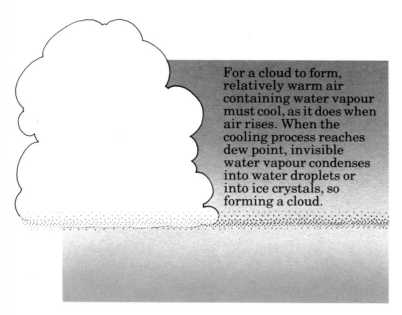

For a cloud to form, relatively warm air containing water vapour must cool, as it does when air rises. When the cooling process reaches dew point, invisible water vapour condenses into water droplets or into ice crystals, so forming a cloud.

The most impressive common cloud is the *Cumulo nimbus*, between 460 m and 2,000 m. Such a cloud may take only half an hour to become 15km deep, boiling up in the sky. It looks like a giant white cauliflower, with brilliant white parts lit by the Sun. From inside the *Cumulo nimbus* come rain, hail and thunderstorms.

How a thundercloud forms

These clouds, like others, form in several ways, due to warm, moist air rising. The cloud may form when air lifts over hills or when a cold front pushes under warmer air, forcing it to rise. Another way is by convection. This happens when air near the ground is warmed by the Sun, expands, gets lighter and rises.

The bubble of warm air rises, carrying moisture with it. The higher it goes, the colder the air becomes. A temperature is reached where the air cannot hold all the invisible water vapour. This temperature is called the dew point. It is at dew point that the invisible water vapour condenses into little droplets of water or crystals of ice, forming a cloud. A *Cumulo nimbus* may look flat at the bottom because it starts to form at the dew point level.

Once the dew point has been passed, the rising air continues to boil upward as a great, visible, towering cloud.

Inside the thundercloud

Inside, tremendous gusts of wind cause great turbulence. While in one part, warm air shoots upward at 20m or 30m per second, in another part, equally violent wind blows downward as rain falls. An aeroplane caught in such a cloud will be flung about.

Finally, the cloud grows so high that it passes the freezing point and the water droplets become ice crystals.

Ways clouds form
Air blowing across the Earth gets turbulent, which may cause it to rise. In the winter, fog over streams or damp fields may lift this way to become *Stratus* cloud.

Convection may occur over man-made 'hot spots' such as cities, where air is warmed by the pavements and buildings. The warm air expands, rises, cools and forms a cloud.

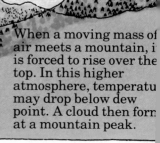

When a moving mass of air meets a mountain, it is forced to rise over the top. In this higher atmosphere, temperature may drop below dew point. A cloud then forms at a mountain peak.

A *Cumulo nimbus* can grow to a height of 15km. At this height, winds tear at the frozen top of the cloud, so that it looks like a giant anvil. Such a cloud may hold more than half-a-million tonnes of water.

If a large mass of cold air meets warm air, it flows under the warm air, forcing it up. This can occur by a coast, where a cool sea breeze meets air warmed by land. A low line of cloud forms.

Rain

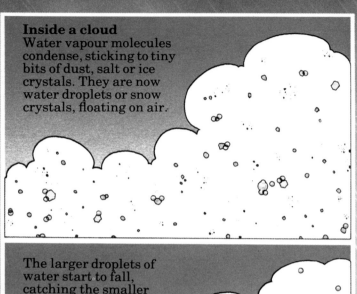

Inside a cloud
Water vapour molecules condense, sticking to tiny bits of dust, salt or ice crystals. They are now water droplets or snow crystals, floating on air.

The larger droplets of water start to fall, catching the smaller droplets on their way. They grow bigger, fall faster and catch even more droplets.

By the time a raindrop leaves a cloud, it is much larger than the tiny droplets in a cloud. The bottom of a raindrop is shaped like an orange that has been flattened.

The atmosphere can carry only a certain amount of water vapour. If the air temperature drops below dew point, so it cannot hold all the invisible water vapour, some of the vapour begins to condense into small droplets, forming a cloud.

Water droplets in a cloud

It is not entirely clear how raindrops form and fall out of a cloud. Molecules of invisible water vapour in the air condense, that is, they stick together on to tiny particles of dust or salt, or round ice crystals at the top of the cloud. The molecules are now bunched together as small water droplets that make up a cloud, floating easily on the air.

How a raindrop is formed

One theory suggests that the slightly larger drops begin to fall and pick up smaller droplets on the way. The larger they get the faster they fall, catching more and more droplets. When the 2mm-diameter raindrop finally leaves the cloud, it is as much as 2,000 times bigger than the tiny cloud droplets. As the raindrop falls, its shape is like an orange flattened at the bottom and not like a tear-drop, as many people imagine.

The importance of rain

People need rain for drinking water for themselves and their animals, as well as for growing their crops. In the broad area south of the Sahara Desert called the Sahel, pastoral tribes manage to survive by grazing their herds of cattle, sheep and goats on sparse vegetation and by hauling water from wells. These people depend on winds from the Atlantic Ocean to carry the only rain that falls on the Sahel.

The monsoons

These winds are called monsoons, which is an Arabic word meaning 'seasonal'. In the hot summer months, air warmed by the continent of Africa rises and moist air sweeps in north-wards from over the ocean to replace it. In the early 1970s the monsoons did not blow. A terrible drought struck the Sahel. Crops could not grow, and hundreds of thousands of people suffered famine, while many of their animals died of starvation.

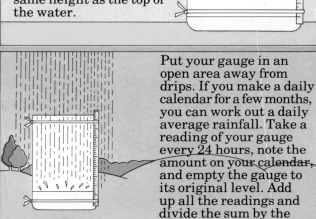

Making a rain gauge

You can make a rough measure of how much rain falls by using a glass with straight sides and a flat bottom. Put enough water in the bottom to cover any curve. With string, tie a ruler with millimetres on it to the side of the glass, so the lowest figure is at the same height as the top of the water.

Put your gauge in an open area away from drips. If you make a daily calendar for a few months, you can work out a daily average rainfall. Take a reading of your gauge every 24 hours, note the amount on your calendar, and empty the gauge to its original level. Add up all the readings and divide the sum by the number of days.

Monsoons are seasonal winds that blow across large areas. In summer they blow from sea to land, bringing heavy rain to areas such as Bangladesh. In winter they blow the other way.

Thunder and lightning

You can forecast a thunderstorm by watching clouds. If the heaps in an *Alto cumulus* grow bigger on a summer afternoon, or if a *Cumulus* cloud grows quickly into a *Cumulo nimbus*, a thunderstorm may be close.

From flash to rumble

Once a storm has broken, you can estimate how far away its centre is. The light from the lightning flash reaches you almost immediately, while the sound of thunder it has caused travels much more slowly – 3km per second. Count the seconds from flash to rumble and divide by three to know how far away the storm is in kilometres. Do this several times to discover if it is getting closer.

Currents in a cloud

Electricity causes lightning. The water droplets and ice crystals that make up a thundercloud have positive charges and negative charges of electricity. A big thundercloud builds up a positive charge at its top and a negative charge at the bottom.

When positive and negative charges of electricity build up near each other, a current tries to flow between them. The ground beneath a thundercloud is positively charged, but the air between the bottom of the cloud and the ground is a good insulator, and so does not carry a current of electricity very well between the cloud and the ground.

Firstly, the cloud sends down a feeler called the leaderstroke. This edges its way through the air, finding the best possible route for an electric current. It finally touches ground at a high point. Then a much more brilliant return stroke leaps back up to the cloud along the leaderstroke's route. It travels at 140,000 km per second – almost half the speed of light. To the eye, this whole process looks like one flash. It is the flow of electric current that has been established between the cloud and the ground.

Buildings are offered some protection by a lightning conductor. This is usually a strip of copper connecting a metal spike on the roof to a metal plate in the ground. It provides lightning with an easy and harmless route to Earth down the outside of the building.

Expanding air

The lightning stroke heats the air, causing it to expand violently. This expansion sends a shock wave through the atmosphere. This shock wave is what we hear echoing round the clouds as thunder.

Safety from lightning Never take shelter under a tree in a thunderstorm. The tree might be the high point that the leaderstroke finds.

Do not stand in an open place, or you might be the high point that is struck. People have survived being struck by lightning but have been burned.

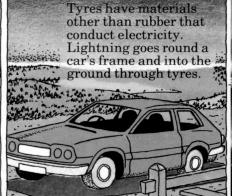

Tyres have materials other than rubber that conduct electricity. Lightning goes round a car's frame and into the ground through tyres.

Fork lightning, which you see leaping between cloud and ground, is 30,000°C at its centre and about 2.5cm wide.

Sheet lightning is simply the reflection of forked lightning that is hidden from an observer by the clouds.

Ball lightning is rare. This 10cm- to 20cm-diameter ball of light floats gently on air, and may finally vanish in a small explosion.

Wild winds

Wind can be a destructive force. Wild winds have various names in different areas round the world.

A cyclone is a large area of low pressure. In the northern hemisphere winds circle the centre in an anti-clockwise direction. South of the equator winds turn the other way. When the winds blow faster than 119 km per hour, the storm is a hurricane.

Hurricanes

Some of the worst hurricanes, in which gusts of wind exceed 350 km per hour, form from cyclones born over tropical seas. Satellite pictures show the swirling patterns of clouds carried by these high winds. Once a hurricane is identified, it is given a name. Its route is then watched carefully, as a hurricane can be very destructive. The word hurricane is from the name of a West Indian storm god. In the Pacific Ocean, these storms are called typhoons, and in Australia they are known as willy willies.

Sand and dust storms

Where there are large stretches of sand or dry earth, turbulent winds that come with some large clouds or with a cold front collect the sand or dust in great billows. In 1933 a storm carried dust from the dry lands of the central plains of the USA as far as the eastern coast. Black rain fell on New York, and brown snow in Vermont.

A satellite photograph shows the centre of a hurricane or cyclone, called an eye. It is about 10km in diameter. The sky in the eye is clear and the wind there is only a breeze.

Sand and dust storms are very unpleasant. Huge clouds of dust or sand carried by the winds block out the Sun, sting people's eyes and smother plant life.

Hurricane Camille knocked down many homes in Gulfport, Mississippi in August 1969. The strong winds that make up the hurricanes can cause wide-spread devastation, uprooting trees and blowing roofs off houses.

As a tornado approaches, it sounds like dozens of roaring express trains. Lightning flickers above, in the cloud from which it hangs. A tornado may tear across the land alone or with others.

Small whirlwinds, no more than a few metres high, often stalk desert sands. Rising pockets of hot air are set spinning by a breeze. Up this twisting funnel of hot air, called a vortex, rises more air carrying dust. Whirlwinds usually last only about three or four minutes. Larger whirlwinds sometimes occur in Arizona in the USA. These can reach 1km in height and last for 30 minutes. The large whirlwinds are capable of causing as much damage as a tornado.

Tornadoes

A tornado is a violently twisting funnel of cloud that extends down to the ground. Tornadoes are associated with intense depressions, large *Cumulo nimbus* clouds or severe cold fronts. They are most frequent in North America.

The winds can spiral round at up to 380 km per hour – faster than any other wind on Earth. The winds twisting up the funnel are strong enough to lift cars, people and trees high into the air. Buildings may be knocked down, or explode as air round them is sucked away. Tornadoes can move at speeds up to 100 km per hour.

Dust devils are small desert whirlwinds. Their upward, cork-screwing motion of air is like the motion of water spiralling down a plug-hole.

Snow and hail

In all the snow that has ever fallen on Earth, it is likely that there have never been two identical snow crystals. Through a magnifying glass, they appear in infinite variations of a few basic patterns.

Crystals of snow

Snow crystals form in a cloud where rising air carries water droplets up to freezing heights. Molecules of water vapour stick to the frozen droplets. These crystals fall and collide with others to form a snowflake. When the crystals are not too cold, they stick together better. This is wet snow, the best sort for making snowballs. The flakes may be 1cm to 2cm in diameter, although flakes 30cm across fell in Siberia in the USSR in 1971.

Where snow falls

In polar regions almost all water vapour falls as snow. The ice caps still contain snow that fell thousands of years ago and which has never melted. In temperate areas of middle latitudes snow falls when the air temperature is near freezing. It rarely falls in latitudes lower than 40° except on high mountains, where the air temperature is cold. It is difficult to measure the depth of snow if there have been high winds, which cause the snow to drift into piles.

six-pointed star

six-pointed star

six-sided flat plate

six-sided flat plate

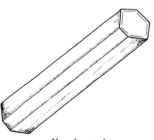
needle-shaped

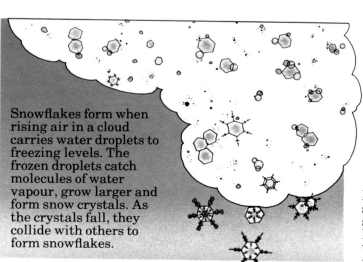
Snowflakes form when rising air in a cloud carries water droplets to freezing levels. The frozen droplets catch molecules of water vapour, grow larger and form snow crystals. As the crystals fall, they collide with others to form snowflakes.

Most snow crystals are six-sided. Some look like six-pointed stars, others like six-sided flat plates while those in another group are needle-shaped.

Snowdrifts on houses or roads can be several metres deep, while fields may be blown almost clear by the wind.

Hail is different from snow. Snow can form in any layered cloud but hail falls only from large *Cumulo nimbus* clouds. Hailstorms are, therefore, most common in mid-latitudes where moist air over land is heated and rises to form these clouds.

Crystals of ice

Hailstones are small pellets of ice. They form when ice crystals from the top of the cloud pick up large drops of super-cooled water. These are water drops that do not freeze, even though the water temperature is below freezing. They do freeze as soon as they touch ice crystals. The ice crystals are carried up and down by the violent winds in the cloud, growing bigger all the time as more droplets freeze to them. Finally, they fall to the ground. Hailstones are usually about the size of a pea.

In 1970, a hailstone measuring 19cm across (about the size of a grapefruit) and weighing 0.75 kg fell in Kansas in the USA. A *Cumulo nimbus* cloud has strong winds to keep a lump of ice suspended in the air long enough to grow that large.

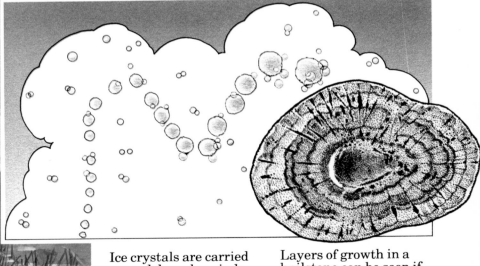

Ice crystals are carried up and down by winds, picking up water drops until they are so heavy they fall from the cloud.

Layers of growth in a hailstone can be seen if one is cut in half and put under a microscope. It resembles an onion.

Dew, frost and fog

Dew forms in the night and evaporates in the warmth of the Sun. On a clear night after a warm day, you can see that dew forms on those materials which radiate their heat away the fastest.

Dew and hoar frost
On a calm night when there are no clouds to keep the warmth in the lower atmosphere, heat quickly radiates away from the ground. Air close to the ground then cools below its dew point, the temperature at which the air is saturated with invisible water vapour. The water vapour in the air condenses into tiny water droplets on any cold surface. This is how dew forms on cobwebs and on grass.

When the dew point is lower than 0°C, the water vapour condenses as ice crystals called hoar frost.

Sometimes dew that is super-cooled (colder than 0°C but still liquid) forms on windows. It later freezes rapidly.

Fog and mist
Fog is simply cloud at ground level. Some meteorologists put the dividing line between fog and mist at about 180 m. If you can see further than 180 m, the cloud is thin enough to be called mist.

Radiation fog
Like other clouds, fog forms when a mass of moist air is cooled below its dew point. This can happen in a number of ways.

When a light breeze stirs air that has been cooled by the ground during the night, the air becomes turbulent. Water vapour then condenses in this cool layer of moist air.

When the first ice crystals of super-cooled dew form on a window, the rest of the dew drops freeze in a rush, spreading beautiful fern patterns across the glass. If you are lucky you may see them form.

The result is patchy cloud at ground level. This is called radiation fog because the ground has radiated away its heat. Such fog forms most often during winter, after long hours of night cooling.

Sea and steam fog

Sea fog forms when warm air is chilled as it blows across the sea's cold surface. Some people in Chile's dry Atacama Desert collect water from sea fog. They have made fog harps which have nylon threads stretched across frames. The sea fog blows from the Pacific Ocean over the harps, and water condenses on the threads. More than 18 litres of water condense on 1sq m per day.

Steam fog floats in cool air over rivers and streams where there is plenty of moisture to keep air saturated with water vapour.

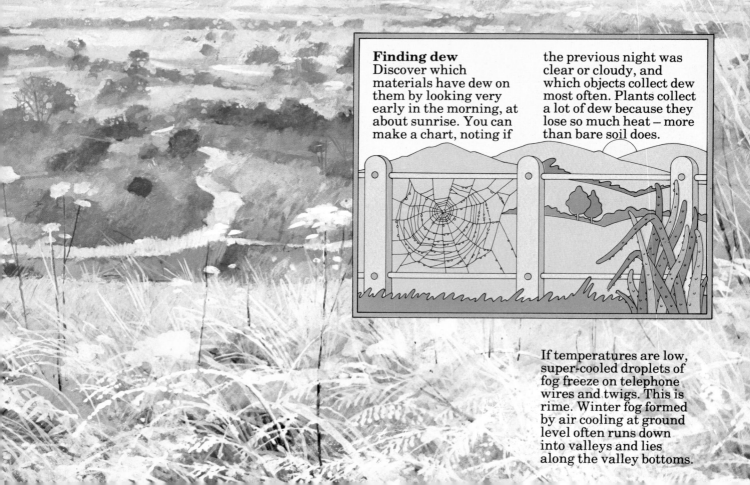

Finding dew
Discover which materials have dew on them by looking very early in the morning, at about sunrise. You can make a chart, noting if the previous night was clear or cloudy, and which objects collect dew most often. Plants collect a lot of dew because they lose so much heat – more than bare soil does.

If temperatures are low, super-cooled droplets of fog freeze on telephone wires and twigs. This is rime. Winter fog formed by air cooling at ground level often runs down into valleys and lies along the valley bottoms.

Tricks of light and colour

Sunlight usually reaches us as white light, but is really a mixture of all the colours of the spectrum — a band of individual colours of red, orange, yellow, green, blue, indigo and violet. The sky looks blue because the atmosphere scatters the blue light in all directions, while it lets the other colours pass straight through to Earth. Special weather conditions may produce colourful, and sometimes even strange, effects.

A rainbow

All the colours of sunlight are seen in a rainbow when the Sun shines behind an observer who is looking into falling rain. As the white sunlight shines into each raindrop, it is bent and split up into the colours of the spectrum. The light then bounces off the inside wall of the raindrop and comes out towards the observer. From one drop, only one of the colours will be at the correct angle to reach the observer. Together, the billions of raindrops build up all the colours in the rainbow.

The arching bow we see is actually part of a complete circle. The lower the Sun is in the sky, the more arc you will see. You might see the whole circle from an aeroplane half-way between the cloud from which the rain is falling and the ground.

Rainbow colours also appear in 'mother of pearl' clouds that float at a height of between 18km and 35km in a twilight sky.

Haloes, mock suns and Sun pillars

White rings called haloes occur round the Sun or Moon when light is refracted, or bent, as it passes through the ice crystals of *Cirro stratus* clouds.

Making a rainbow
You can make a rainbow by using the fine spray of a garden hose. Stand with your back to the Sun when it is low in the sky. It helps if you face a dark-coloured object, such as a bush. Rainbows can be seen in the same way in the mist from a fountain's spray.

Haloes round the Sun or Moon are not uncommon sights. The fuller and brighter the Moon, the clearer the halo will be.

Sun pillars and mock suns are less common sights than haloes. Mock suns may have rainbow colours in them.

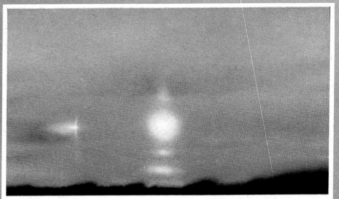

Mock suns look almost like the real Sun. They are caused in the same sort of way as haloes, and can be seen on either side of the Sun or both sides.

A column of light above or beneath the Sun is called a Sun pillar. It is caused by reflection of light from ice crystals.

Mirages

A mirage is an optical illusion. Some mirages are seen in the air when objects beyond the horizon, such as mountains, appear in the wrong positions. Others are seen on the ground. A mirage occurs when light is bent as it passes from dense, cold air into a layer of warm air, or the other way round. Distant objects then look distorted or appear where they do not belong.

Hot air over a desert or road has a layer of denser, cold air just above it, and so is a common place for a mirage to occur. The light from the sky is reflected as though by a mirror, from the warm layer of air above the road. It looks like water.

Sometimes a fainter, second bow is seen above the main rainbow. When this occurs, the order of colours in the second bow is always reversed.

The illusion of water shimmering on dry ground is a common mirage. The 'water' disappears as you approach it.

Winds and waves

Sea hazards

Water spouts form where the cork-screwing and violent action of wind beneath a *Cumulo nimbus* cloud sucks up water and spray from the surface of the sea.

Icebergs are giant slabs of ice and compact snow that break away from the northern or southern ice caps in warm weather and drift slowly with ocean currents, melting as they go.

Freezing spray and fog can capsize a small boat when they freeze on the deck and rigging. If the boat is covered in a thick layer of ice, the weight might cause the boat to topple over.

The weather at sea may be an enemy or a friend. Seafarers have always been at the mercy of sea fogs, icebergs, freak waves, storms and water spouts. On the other hand, sailors use the wind over seas to carry their ships across water, either for trade, as in the days of great sailing ships, or for pleasure.

Sea winds

In fact, mariners named some of the regular winds that blow across oceans. The trade winds blowing towards the equator from the north-east in the northern hemisphere, and from the south-east in the southern hemisphere, carried great trading ships from continent to continent. The 'roaring forties' are westerly winds that blow 40° south of the equator, tearing across the southern Atlantic and Pacific Oceans where there is no land

Dangerous freak waves are unpredictable and, luckily, they are also rare. Waves travel over the sea at different speeds. When one wave meets another or crosses it at an angle, they may combine for a moment to create a giant wave.

mass to slow them down. At the equator, the doldrums left sailing ships becalmed, because winds there are light or non-existent.

Winds cause waves

Waves are caused by wind blowing across the sea's surface. Blow across a basin of water and you can see this happen. Without wind the sea would be calm and the tides would creep silently up and down the beach with hardly a splash. The stronger the wind, the higher the waves.

When a few white horses appear, the wind speed is about 10 knots. A knot is equal to 1.852 km per hour. White horses are the tops of waves being blown over by the breeze and breaking with a splash of spray. A moderate breeze of 11 to 16 knots covers the sea with white horses. A strong gale of 41 to 47 knots

can produce waves 10m high, while in a hurricane, the force of the wind may produce waves as high as 20m.

The giant barometer

Atmospheric pressure also affects the sea. The sea acts as a sort of giant barometer. When air pressure is high, the weight of the heavy air forces the sea level down so that both high and low tides are lower than they would be normally.

The reverse happens during a period of low pressure, or a deep depression, lightening the load of air on the sea. When this occurs together with strong winds blowing behind the rising tide, it can cause a tide to be as much as 2.5 m higher than usual. This kind of high tide is called a storm surge, and it will flood many low-lying coastal areas.

Storm surges occur only along low-lying coasts, causing severe floods such as those experienced by towns on the east coast of England in 1953.

Microclimates

Meteorologists talk about the 'microclimate' when describing local conditions, meaning the climate of a small area.

A city microclimate

A city helps to create its own climate. The rock, brick and concrete store the Sun's heat. They act like radiators, warming the air round them. Factories, heating systems and vehicles add more warmth. Dust and smoke pollution also keep up the temperature. When there is no wind or rain, a dome-shaped layer of dust covers the city in a haze, trapping heat. Buildings give protection from

wind, which helps keep air warmer. A city's night temperature may be 8°C warmer than surrounding countryside, from the release of all this trapped heat.

A city affects the country

Sulphur dioxide is one pollutant produced by factories, homes and vehicles. When dissolved in rain, it forms dilute sulphuric acid, which falls back on the city or on the countryside downwind. It is corrosive and poisonous, eating away at stonework and metal, and even killing plants and animals.

Country microclimates

Microclimates away from a city are affected by natural elements. Woodland cuts down wind speed. It also helps keep air cooler at

Cities help make their own climates because of buildings, while rural climates are shaped more by natural forces.

ground level on a summer's day. A river may also keep down the day's temperature, since air over water heats more slowly than air over land. The temperature of an area may be raised by certain kinds of soil, such as sand, which radiate more heat than other kinds. A town by the sea will have more breezes than an inland town, because wind is sometimes caused by cool air over seas replacing warm air over land.

Hills and valleys

Houses in the bottom of a valley, although protected from gales, may be in the cold shadow of hills. On a calm night the valley bottom may be colder than the hilltops, because cold air, which is heavier than warm air, may run down from the hilltops into the valley below. Gardens at the valley bottom are then in a frost hollow, and will have more frosty nights than gardens that are up on the open hillside.

Houses on hilltops have disadvantages, too. Winter snow lies on the hilltops longer than in valleys, and there are more gales. Cold air and rain penetrate exposed houses more easily.

A good position for a house is between a hilltop and the bottom of the valley. Avoiding frost hollows, it may still be sheltered from the worst winds. If a house in the northern hemisphere faces south it will get a lot of Sun.

Plants prove pollution
Lichens are primitive plants that absorb the sulphuric acid in rain. Some lichens die where air is polluted, others can survive. You can see how polluted air is by which lichens you find and where they grow.

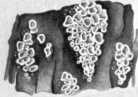

Look for *Lecanora dispersa* on concrete, walls, limestone and paving stones in areas that are polluted.

Look for *Hypogymnia pysodes* on bases of tree trunks in clean air and higher on trees in areas that are polluted.

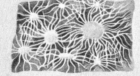

Look for *Usnea florida* growing on trees and sometimes on rocks in areas with clean air, such as the countryside.

Past climates

Some of the earliest legends are about un-expected changes in the weather. About 6,000 years ago a huge flood hit the cities of Sumeria, north of the area now called the Persian Gulf. Storytellers said that their gods had sent the floods to destroy mankind, because they could not sleep with all the noise on Earth. This is recorded on clay tablets in the 'Epic of Gilgamesh', a famous Babylonian poem.

Effects of climate

History has been affected by climate. About 1,000 years ago, for instance, there was a warm spell, and there were fewer storms in the Atlantic Ocean and North Sea. The Vikings were able to sail the oceans and colonise Iceland and Greenland, and even travel as far as North America.

Collecting past information

Meteorologists all round the world collect information about patterns of change in the Earth's climate from different sources. Many sources of information, when used together, build up a general picture of the world's weather and climate.

Discovering the past
Some bristle-cone pines of California are 4,000 years old. These, along with older, dead timber, give a weather record for the past 8,000 years.

Scientists drill for layers of compressed snow in the Antarctic or in Greenland. The dust and volcanic ash that fell with the snow show past atmospheric pollution.

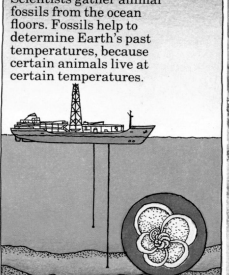

Scientists gather animal fossils from the ocean floors. Fossils help to determine Earth's past temperatures, because certain animals live at certain temperatures.

During the last Ice Age, glaciers of ice extended across Britain, Holland, Scandinavia and parts of Germany. These glaciers created small icebergs. Primitive lichens grew on bare rocks in this bleak landscape.

One source that is useful is the analysis of tree rings. A tree adds a new ring of growth for each year it lives. Thin rings show years of poor growth, suggesting droughts or severe spring frosts.

Meteorologists also use a drill with a hollow centre to bring up long, rod-shaped ice cores dating back 100,000 years. They have discovered a link between volcanic activity and cold spells on Earth.

Drills also collect samples from ocean floors. Animal fossils found in the samples give information about temperatures of the oceans dating back 100 million years.

The recent past

There have been four great Ice Ages in the last 1,000 million years. The most recent of these ended about 10,000 years ago. Since then, there has been a slight warming trend, sometimes called an interglacial period. However, from 1550 to 1850 there was a cold period known as the Little Ice Age. There are many written records, including diaries, of this time. The climate has warmed since 1850, but there are indications that this Little Ice Age is not over yet. By studying past climates, meteorologists hope to discover patterns of changes that will help predict the future.

Signs of the Ice Ages are seen in some large rocks. Glaciers carved these rocks, which have one smooth, rounded side and one rough side with a steep slope.

Forecasting the weather

Folklore is full of sayings that attempt to forecast weather, for instance:

> 'Red sky at night, shepherd's delight;
> Red sky in the morning,
> shepherd's warning.'

An experienced amateur can guess what the weather will be like for the next few hours, or perhaps days. But a prediction cannot be made on a single bit of information, such as the sky's colour, because the weather system is world-wide. Local weather affects weather in other places, so a forecast depends on accurate knowledge of weather in many areas. World weather must be studied as one great system.

Meteorologists in different countries exchange information, which makes it easier to build a world-wide weather picture.

Instruments help

Weather conditions change quickly, so it is important to collect information swiftly. Scientists use trained observers and instruments to collect data on air pressure, temperature, rainfall, clouds and wind.

Two sorts of satellites contribute to global weather patterns. Those on a polar orbit circle the Earth every two hours, recording information on the temperature and moisture of the air at different heights.

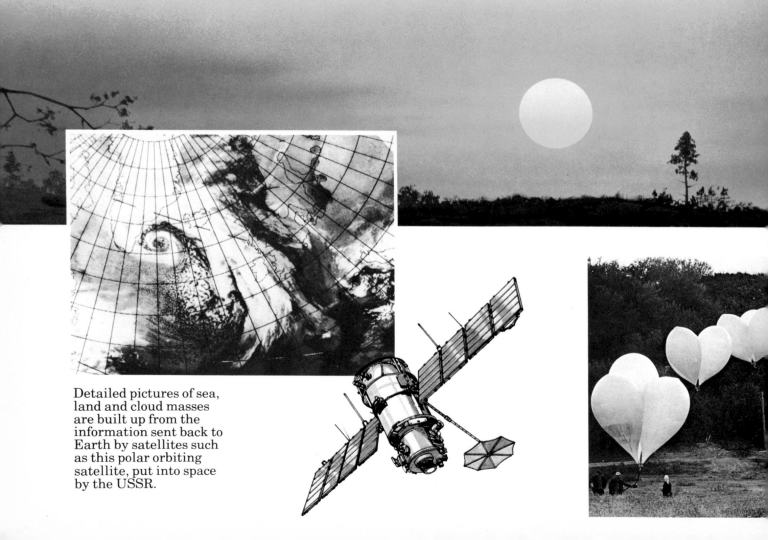

Detailed pictures of sea, land and cloud masses are built up from the information sent back to Earth by satellites such as this polar orbiting satellite, put into space by the USSR.

The other sort, geo-stationary satellites, are launched to 33,000 km. They remain at the same spot above the equator, because they keep up with the speed of the Earth's rotation. Their cameras record air currents and cloud formation.

The importance of forecasting

All this information, gathered from round the world, builds up a picture of each day's weather. This enables meteorologists to make a forecast. It is possible, however, that this forecast may be incorrect. This is because all the ways in which the atmosphere works are not understood entirely. More information is needed before forecasts can be more accurate.

Weather forecasting can, however, take some of the uncertainty out of planning ahead on a short-term basis. Motorists can be told of fog or icy roads. Ships and aircraft can be warned of storms, fog, snow and ice. Farmers benefit from forecasts of frosts or storms that might destroy a harvest. Governments forewarned of temporary climatic changes, such as droughts, can make plans to protect people from famine. Even bakers can benefit from forecasts – it seems that people in Europe buy more bread and cakes in sudden cold spells.

If not too much cloud is on the horizon, a red sky at night is probably due to atmospheric dust and may mean good weather. An angry, deep-red glow on the underside of thick clouds may mean rain.

Trained observers at weather stations in the USSR (left) launch weather balloons filled with hydrogen. These carry instruments to a certain level of the atmosphere, recording weather as they drift. Like most stations, this one collects data about the lower atmosphere.

People in the Sahel near the Sahara Desert may be able to save cattle from starvation (right), if warned of droughts.

Changing the weather

People's earliest attempts at changing the weather were tribal dances, sacrifices and offerings to their gods. The Cheyenne tribe of the North American Indians, for instance, performed a four-day Sun dance at midsummer to control the weather.

Today, people's experiments for changing the climate are more scientific. No one can make rain fall from a blue sky, but clouds offer more hope.

Seeding clouds

A chemical called silver iodide has been used in many countries to force clouds to release their moisture.

Either silver iodide or frozen carbon dioxide crystals, known as dry ice, are sprayed into a likely-looking cloud by rocket or aircraft. This process is called seeding, because water drops are believed to 'grow' round the carbon dioxide crystals or silver iodide until they are so large that they fall out of the cloud as raindrops.

There is disagreement about how effective this method actually is, because it can always be said that rain would have fallen from these clouds anyway.

When silver iodide is sprayed into clouds, the super-cooled drops of water freeze. The ice crystals fall out of the cloud, leaving a hole.

If hailstones are left to grow in a cloud, they can be very destructive. A field of crops can be completely ruined by one storm in a very short time. Seeding clouds is one experiment that can help farmers.

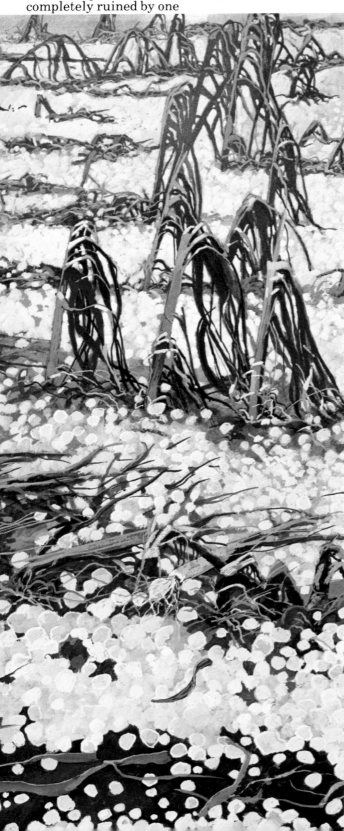

At any rate, only certain kinds of clouds respond to this expensive process. People are still a long way from being able to create rain whenever and wherever they choose.

Preventing hailstorms

Equally uncertain are the results of experiments to prevent hail from destroying crops. Some people think that if explosive shells containing silver iodide are fired into likely clouds, the hailstones will not have time to grow before they fall.

Small-scale experiments

Another experiment is the clearing of fog from roads and airport runways. Silver iodide or salt crystals have been used to turn the fog into rain. Heaters aimed at fog on runways have caused fog to lift.

Other ideas, such as building windbreaks and erecting lightning conductors, have proved effective. But so far, all that people have managed to do is to modify local weather, with small-scale changes.

Scientists in the USSR claim success at turning hail into rain. As soon as *Cumulo nimbus* clouds are spotted, shells from anti-hail rockets are fired into them, forcing the clouds to rain.

The future

People are interfering with the climate in ways that may be unintentional, but the changes that take place certainly will have long-term and world-wide effects.

Another Ice Age

Mankind is filling the atmosphere with dust from chimneys, vehicles' exhausts and from 'dust bowls', where poor farming methods have laid the land bare for wind to blow away soil. One theory argues that this 'human volcano' condition will cut off some of the Sun's heat that reaches Earth, causing the atmosphere to cool enough for a new Ice Age to begin.

Between 1940 and 1970 the temperature of the northern hemisphere dropped, on average, about 0.5°C, suggesting that this cooling process might be starting. Imagine a wall of ice more than 1km thick, sliding over Europe or the USA.

A warm spell

On the other hand, we may be entering a warm period, with no ice at the polar regions. Some scientists argue that by burning so much coal and oil, we are filling the atmosphere with carbon dioxide. This would trap some of the Sun's heat and warm up the world's climate. Cutting down tropical rain forests, such as those in Brazil, may have the same result. Since 1850 the amount of carbon dioxide in the atmosphere has actually increased by 10%.

With a world-wide weather watch we may soon know in which direction our climate is heading. Either way, our future will be affected greatly by actions we take now.

If the world's climate gets warmer and the ice caps melt, the sea level will rise slowly by as much as 90m, flooding coastal cities such as London and New York. Sand, carried by the tides, would soon pile up round the crumbling buildings.

Charting the weather

The Beaufort wind scale for use on land

Force	Description	Specifications for use on land	Average km per hour
0	Calm	Smoke rises vertically	0
1	Light air	Wind direction shown by smoke drift, not vanes	3.2
2	Light breeze	Wind felt on face, leaves rustle, vane moved by wind	8
3	Gentle breeze	Leaves, twigs in constant motion, light flag extends	16
4	Moderate breeze	Dust, loose paper raised, small branches move	24
5	Fresh breeze	Small trees in leaf sway, crested wavelets on inland waters	33.6
6	Strong breeze	Large branches move, telegraph wires whistle	44.8
7	Near gale	Whole trees move, inconvenient to walk against wind	56
8	Gale	Twigs break off trees, wind impedes movement	67.6
9	Strong gale	Chimney pots and slates removed from roofs	80.4
10	Storm	Considerable structural damage, trees uprooted	94.9
11	Violent storm	Wide-spread damage	109.4
12	Hurricane	Devastation	more than 119

World weather extremes

Hottest place: Dallol, Ethiopia
Coldest place: Polus Nedostupnosti, Antarctica
Driest place: Atacama Desert, Chile
Wettest place: Mount Wai-'ale-'ale, Kauai, Hawaii
Most thundery place: Bogor, Java, Indonesia
Windiest place: George V Coast, Antarctica
Places where tornadoes most frequent: mid-west USA

Freaks of weather

Largest hailstone: 190 mm-diameter in Kansas, USA
Highest recorded wave: 26m in Atlantic Ocean
Highest observed wave: 34m in Pacific Ocean
Highest recorded water spout: 1,528 m off Australia
Deepest measured frozen ground: 1,500 m in Siberia
Highest recorded wind gust: 371 km per hour, in Mt Washington, USA

Measuring humidity

Measure humidity with a hair. Using scissors, cut out a rectangular shape 20cm × 6cm from a piece of card. Bend and tape it to the back of another rectangular card 20cm × 12cm, as a prop. Cut out a paper arrow. Pin the straight end near the bottom of the card.

Tape one end of a long hair to the card above the point. Tape the other end to the point. The hair will lengthen on humid days and will shorten on dry days, moving the arrow. Write 'damp' and 'dry' next to the places it stops. In a few weeks you will be able to see how humid a day is.

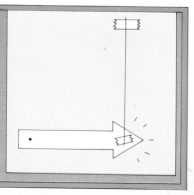

Index

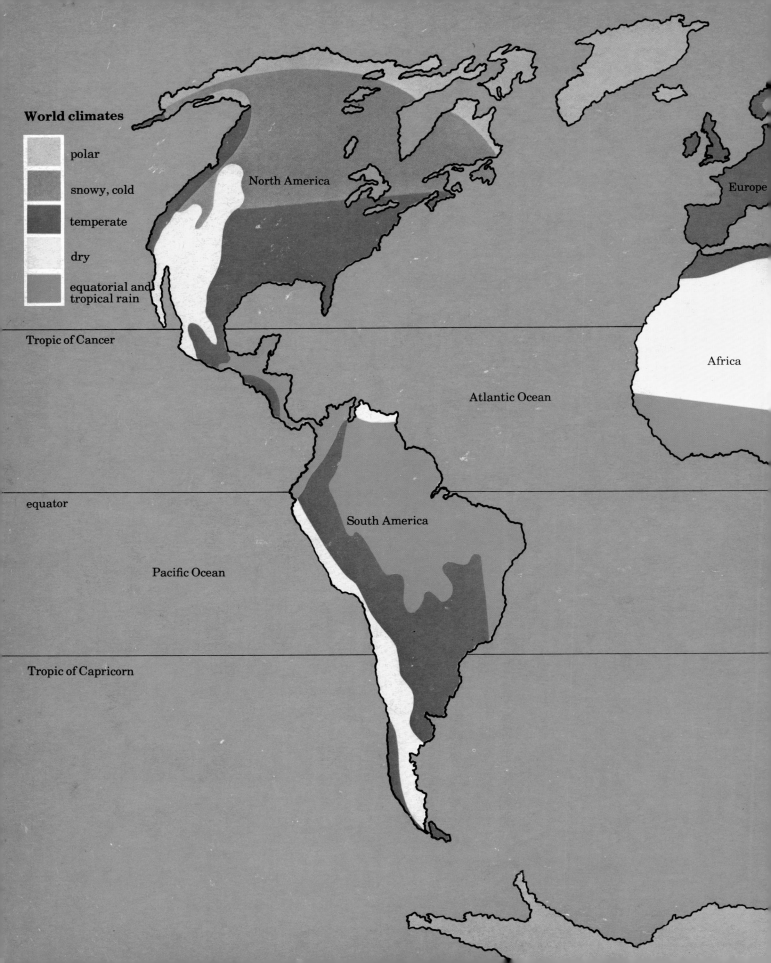

World climates

polar

snowy, cold

temperate

dry

equatorial and
tropical rain

North America

Europe

Tropic of Cancer

Africa

Atlantic Ocean

equator

South America

Pacific Ocean

Tropic of Capricorn